For Lily Rose with love **K.S.**

Text by Sophie Piper
Illustrations copyright © 2008 Kristina Stephenson
This edition copyright © 2008 Lion Hudson

The moral rights of the author and illustrator
have been asserted

A Lion Children's Book
an imprint of
Lion Hudson plc
Wilkinson House, Jordan Hill Road,
Oxford OX2 8DR, England
www.lionhudson.com
UK ISBN: 978 0 7459 6115 6
US ISBN: 978 0 8254 7887 1

First edition 2008
This printing June 2009
10 9 8 7 6 5 4 3 2 1

Typeset in 20/24 Baskerville MT Schoolbook
Printed and bound in China by Main Choice

Distributed by:
UK: Marston Book Services Ltd, PO Box 269, Abingdon, OX14 4YN
USA: Trafalgar Square Publishing, 814 N Franklin Street, Chicago, IL
60610
USA Christian Market: Kregel Publications, PO Box 2607, Grand
Rapids, MI 49501

The Angel and the Lamb

Sophie Piper

Illustrations by Kristina Stephenson

LION
CHILDREN'S

The little lamb squeezed close to his shepherd boy.
The road to Bethlehem had never been this busy
before!

'What's going on?' his shepherd boy asked.

'Everyone has to go and put their names on a list,' came the reply. 'The emperor wants a list of tax payers.'

When the road was clear, Ben the shepherd boy walked on, with his lamb and his flock behind him.

'I'm glad we won't be in Bethlehem tonight,' said Ben. 'It will be so crowded. We'll be out on the hillside, under the stars.'

Already a bright star was shining in the sunset sky.

Suddenly, Little Lamb had an idea. Perhaps it would be more fun to go to Bethlehem.

Without really thinking, he skipped behind a thorn bush and waited till the flock had passed.

Then he ran.
And ran.

And ran.

He ran as fast and as
far as he could.

Already he could hear Ben calling for him. But he knew Ben couldn't see him.
All he had to do was wait.

Then he could go down
the road to Bethlehem.

Ben walked slowly down the
hillside and up the next. Then he
went back to the other shepherds.
'I can't find my lamb,' he said. 'Can you
watch my sheep while I go looking?'

The shepherds shook their heads. 'It's dangerous to go roaming the hills at night,' they said. 'We can go in the morning.'

As the last drop of the sun's rosy light slipped below the hills, the world went dark.

Little Lamb was not on the road to Bethlehem.
Little Lamb had tumbled into a prickly hollow.

It went dark.

Little Lamb could hear
hooting and howling.

He could hear
snuffling and
snarling.

He could see sly shapes slinking
slowly nearer.
And the eyes! The eyes!

All at once, there was a swirl of light,
bright as a waterfall, warm as the sunshine.

Were they really
angels?

'Can I help you?' asked a voice.
    It was an angel, no taller than Ben.

But the voice was more musical than a flute.
    From the angel's golden curls shone a clear light
that scattered the darkness.

'Come with me,' said the angel. 'I know where you will be safe.'

The angel led Little Lamb down the hill and up the hill and along the road to Bethlehem.

There, in a tiny room, among the animals, were the two passers-by to whom Ben had spoken.

The woman was holding a baby, newly born.

'Hello, Little Lamb,' said the mother. 'Are you looking for home?'

Through the door came Ben and the other
shepherds.

'We saw angels!' cried Ben. 'They said we'd
find a baby… and here he is.'

'And here is a lamb,' said the mother. 'Was he lost?'

'He was,' said Ben, 'and I'm so glad to have found him.'

The angel slipped back into the night sky as Ben carried Little Lamb closer to the baby and smiled.